Mungo

Wordsworth

by Rosalie K. Fry

*Promise of the Rainbow*

*Whistler in the Mist*

*Snowed Up*

*Mungo*

*Farrar, Straus & Giroux* • *New York*

# Rosalie K. Fry

# Mungo

illustrated by Velma Ilsley

Mungo

Richie ducked down into the heather so that he would not be seen as he crawled to the edge of the cliff and wormed his way down an overgrown track to the secret bay below. It was his own special private place, hidden from above by the overhanging heather and screened from the sea by a tall rock pillar that stood on the shore. The base of the pillar was ringed with a fringe of seaweed, and a cushion of sea pinks grew on top.

There were other great rocks along this rugged coast of Scotland, but this was Richie's favorite because it not only hid his secret bay but also served as a lookout tower from which he could keep watch. For he had discovered tracks on the shore—strange tracks, as though some tremendous creature had come blundering into his bay from the sea and then gone blundering out again. And only yesterday Richie had found a tussock of grass torn up by the roots and dropped on the edge of the tide. There was no doubt about it, something very odd was going on.

He climbed up and lay flat on the sea-pink cushion now, trying to look like part of the rock. His green shirt, faded shorts, and sunburned arms and legs were fine, and he hoped his yellow hair might pass for a tuft of sun-bleached grass if he kept still enough.

For a while he did keep still, only his gray eyes moving as he scanned the restless sea. But he soon forgot about keeping watch and turned to look at the bell buoy as it plunged and rolled in the tumbling surge of the tide rip. He loved that bell buoy with its mellow *clang-clung . . . clang-clung,* warning shipping day and night, *"Keep clear . . . keep clear . . . keep clear . . ."*

He was so busy not thinking what he was doing that he upset the bag of potato crisps he had brought to eat on watch, and only realized what had happened when he saw a handful of the crinkled flakes floating like yellow petals on the sea below. One minute they were there, bobbing among the rocks, and the next minute—*shloooooop* —they were slowly sucked out of sight.

"That . . . rock . . . ate . . . my crisps!" Richie stammered, almost toppling into the sea himself as he craned forward to gape at one of the rounded humps in the swirling sea. A wave swept up around it, and as it poured over the smooth dark shape, he caught his breath and stared again. For a moment it looked more like a head than a rock. He even fancied he saw two eyes, but before he could be certain, another wave broke over it, smothering it in foam.

"Oh, bother these old waves. How can I see when they keep getting in the way?" he cried impatiently, slithering down from his high perch to stand on the flat wet rocks below.

Fortunately the tide was on the turn, and as the waves fell back, bit by bit a comical face began to emerge, comic but nice, with small bright eyes and a silly soft smile that made Richie want to laugh.

He followed the falling tide, hopping from one newly uncovered rock to another, until he was standing directly above the oddest-looking creature he had ever seen. It lay wallowing in the surf, lazily lifting its head from time to time to nibble a little seaweed off the surrounding rocks, watching him all the while with a friendly glint in its sleepy eyes.

As the waves sucked back, Richie saw that it had a long, smooth neck, thickening into a hummocky body that stretched out into the sea like a low reef of rocks.

"And most of it must be rocks. No animal could be *that* long!"

He said the words out loud to convince himself as a sudden shiver trickled down his spine. He turned back hastily to the nice foolish face, which was a much more comfortable size, some-

thing between a St. Bernard dog and a horse.

"Only it's not like the shape of a dog or a horse," he mused. "More like a kind of giant lizard with the longest neck in the world!"

He was just wondering if it would understand like a dog if he spoke to it, when his attention was caught by the sound of the bell buoy. Its *clang-clung* had become so much a part of the background of his life that he rarely noticed it, but now it seemed to have an added note, turning the sound into *clang-clung-CLONG* . . . *clang-clung-CLONG* . . . He glanced across to where it rocked among the white-capped waves,

but it looked just as usual, and he soon turned back to the great beast in the sea at his feet.

But something strange was happening. The smiling face was turned away, and the long body seemed to be moving too, churning the water into wild commotion as the waves fell over one another in a sudden swirl of foam. Here and there dark humps rose out of the tumbled sea, but they looked like perfectly ordinary rocks to Richie.

"But he was here, I didn't dream him, I know I didn't," he muttered fiercely. "I saw him and he saw me, and we liked each other too."

The tide was ebbing rapidly now, uncovering new stretches of flat rock. But in the entrance to the secret bay, where the strange great beast had wallowed, it uncovered nothing but an empty gully with a floor of fine white shingle. He wandered about between the brimming rock pools, waiting and watching as the tide went out, but nothing further happened. Even the bell buoy sounded just as usual.

"And I didn't imagine that bit either!" he shouted over the sea. "I heard you going *clang-clung-CLONG*, no matter what you're doing now!"

Suddenly he found himself longing to talk about what he had seen and heard with someone who would understand. But there was nobody except himself and Aunt Hilda, and it wasn't the sort of thing one could expect a grownup to believe. Besides, since coming to cook at the Cliff Hotel, Aunt Hilda was always busy, especially during the summer.

This didn't trouble Richie as a rule. He saw plenty of people at school and enjoyed puttering about on his own during the holidays, free from teasing voices calling "Wake up, Richie!" Because he wasn't asleep at all of course, only planning marvelous adventures. So he welcomed the timeless peace of the holidays, when he was free to wander about in a daydream, with only the sea and the undemanding gulls for company.

But now for the first time he felt the need of a friend. Well, he decided, if he couldn't tell anyone what he had seen, he could at least ask questions—careful questions! Cheered by this idea, he scrambled up the heathery cliff and hurried along a sheep track until he came in sight of the hotel.

Chapter Two

Aunt Hilda was in the scullery, helping Jeannie with the washing up. She and Richie could only smile and wink at one another because Jeannie was describing her sister's wedding, and Richie knew better than to try to interrupt such a conversation.

A pleasant warm smell of ironing reminded him that it was one of Mrs. Moffatt's days, and he went through into the back kitchen, where she was ironing sheets on the long deal table. He liked the days when Mrs. Moffatt came to do the laundry. She always had a welcoming smile for him and sensible answers to his questions, much more sensible than Jeannie's.

Mrs. Moffatt had done a lot for Richie since he came to live in Scotland. In the early days poor Aunt Hilda, unused to country life herself, had fussed and fretted over him. It was then that Mrs. Moffatt had come to his rescue.

He remembered the day so vividly. They had been out by the clothesline, Mrs. Moffatt and Aunt Hilda hanging out the sheets, while he stood by with the pegs. It was a wonderful day in early autumn, with white clouds flying before a leaping wind. The wet sheets seemed to be trying to fly before it too. Richie smiled to himself, imagining how they must feel as they tugged at the pegs, straining to be free. The sound of Mrs. Moffatt's voice had brought him out of his reverie with a jerk.

"The child will never lose that pinched white look if you keep him tied to your apron strings, my dear," she was saying in her kindly, forthright manner. "Freedom is what he's needing. There comes a time when you've got to let them go free or they'll never learn to look after themselves. It's hard for you, I know that only too well." And she put an understanding hand on Aunt Hilda's shoulder as she went on. "I'm sure you'll find you can trust your Richie, just as I trusted my own Angus when he was a lad. I let him go free on the understanding that he'd be home by a certain time—"

"Ah, but Richie hasn't got a watch," objected Aunt Hilda.

"Who said anything about watches?" demanded Mrs. Moffatt. "There's ways of telling the time without watches. And you needn't look so alarmed, Richie boy!" she chuckled. "I'm not expecting you to tell the time by the sun! There's a simpler way than that. I'm sure you've noticed the steamer that passes down the coast around 5:30 every evening?"

"I know, with a yellow funnel!" burst out Richie.

"That's the one and that's all the watch my Angus ever had. When he saw that steamer coming, he knew he'd to be home before she was out of sight. Luckily her route lies a long way out from the shore, so she's in sight for quite a while."

"And what if she was late?" questioned Aunt Hilda doubtfully.

"Och well, I knew what time she was due, you see. So I'd only to go to the window, and if she wasn't in sight I'd know she'd been held up. Of course there were foggy days, I'd have to make allowances then.

"Mind you," she went on with a twinkle, "there were times when I was afraid my wild young Angus was going to let me down. But just as I was beginning to wonder, he'd come panting in from the shore with his hair on end and the smell of the sea about him."

"The smell of the sea sounds exciting," said Richie. "What did he do on the shore?"

Mrs. Moffatt shook her head with a smile as she replied. "He never told me. He was always one to be on his own, was Angus."

"And where is he now?" Aunt Hilda asked.

"He's a lighthouse keeper. It's a grand job, for all it's kind of lonely, and it certainly suits him fine."

"A lighthouse keeper!" breathed Richie with shining eyes. Perhaps one day he, too, might become a lighthouse keeper, in charge of one of those flashing lights that winked across the sea at night.

"Is it one we can see from here?" he demanded eagerly.

"It is indeed, it's the one with the four quick

flashes out there beyond the headland. You can see it from your bedroom. I love that light, it's company, like it might be Angus himself waving over the water!" And she gave a little laugh as she stooped to lift another sodden sheet from the basket. But when she turned for a clothes peg Richie was already lost in a dream, picturing the boy Angus roaming the coast, timing his days by a yellow-funneled steamer. And now he, Richie, was to roam this same coast himself! Perhaps at last he would have a real adventure . . .

He had lost no time in making the most of his new freedom, setting out at once to explore the cliffs and shoreline until eventually he discovered the secret bay.

At first he wondered if he was the only person in the world who knew the bay was there. Then he came upon the strange tracks in the shingle, and today he had seen something that sent him scurrying home without even waiting for the steamer to appear.

"You're back early," commented Mrs. Moffatt, looking at him in surprise.

"Am I?" said Richie lightly, hoping he sounded calmer than he felt. Then, taking a deep breath, he began cautiously: "I suppose there must be heaps of simply enormous creatures in the sea out there?"

"Well, now, I don't rightly know," she replied thoughtfully, folding a sheet and smoothing out the wrinkles. "I wouldn't say all that big. I suppose seals would be about the biggest round here."

"Seals!" he exclaimed disappointedly. "The ones I've seen aren't much bigger than me."

"Ah, but a real grand old bull seal would be a sight larger than that."

"How big then? As long as from here to the gate?"

"Oh, go on with you! Are you looking for the Loch Ness Monster?" She laughed, reaching for the iron.

Richie decided that this conversation had gone quite far enough, so he wandered across to the window in search of a change of subject.

Although his secret bay and its guardian rock could not be seen from the hotel, there was an exciting view of the coastline, with its offshore rocks and skerries rising out of a tumble of white surf. He looked searchingly from rock to rock, but with the whole wild sea in motion it was easy to imagine that half the humped dark shapes were moving. However, the larger ones were steady enough, and he murmured the names of those he knew, until his eye was caught by his favorite, Muckle Craig, rearing up on its own, way out beyond the bell buoy. He turned from the window with a new question.

"Do boats ever go out to Muckle Craig and all those other islands?"

"Islands!" Mrs. Moffatt chuckled. "That lot's no more than skerries. Nobody wants to go out to those."

"I would," said Richie boldly.

"Well, you can't, that's all," she said decidedly. "Nobody's ever set foot on Muckle Craig and nobody ever will. You've only to look at the wicked old tide rip roaring through the sound there. No boat ever built could stay right side up in that, leastways no boat that was small enough to make its way between the skerries."

"What about on calm days?"

"It's never calm out there. That's what the bell buoy's put there for, to keep the boats away."

Richie said no more. But he had the strangest feeling that some day, somehow, he was going to land on Muckle Craig.

Chapter Three

Richie was down in his secret bay long before breakfast next morning, and there he remained all day, only dashing up reluctantly to eat his meals as quickly as he could.

But although he followed the ebbing tide, prowling all over the newly uncovered rocks, there was no sign of the great beast of yesterday. He examined the gully in which he had seen it, but the shingle floor was smooth and the rocky sides covered with whelks and anemones, as though no great body had ever wallowed there.

"But I know he was here. I saw him," Richie muttered obstinately.

All through the long bright afternoon he watched the tide come stealing in again, until the gully and its surrounding rocks were covered. When the waves came lapping around the base of the rock pillar and into the secret bay, he climbed to his lookout post and lay among the sea pinks. He had brought a bag of potato crisps just in case, and this time he was careful not to spill them as he screwed up his eyes against the dazzle of sunlit water, scanning the sea for a sign of the beast.

And then, quite suddenly, there it was! At one time he would have thought it no more than a reef of rocks, but now he recognized the shape of the sleek head and could just glimpse the good-natured smile between the breaking waves.

Clutching the bag of crisps in one hand, he began to climb down the side of the rock, moving very quietly so as not to alarm the creature lying in the sea below.

But the creature was not in the least alarmed, and by the time Richie reached the flat rocks the long neck was already arching out of the water, the head looking curiously small on its great length of neck. For a moment it swung from side to side as though in search of something, while the water streamed from its comical face, making it appear to be dribbling hopefully. Then Richie saw it stiffen as it spotted the bag of crisps he was holding, and slowly, slowly, slowly the long neck

stretched out toward him until he could see two
small, glinting, sea-green eyes fixed eagerly upon
the bag in his hand.

When he saw that the creature was not afraid
of him, he determined that, in spite of its alarming size, he must not be frightened either. So he
ripped open the bag and scattered a shower of
crisps on the rocks around his feet. Then he
forced himself to stand perfectly still while the
great beast stooped to suck them up, slowly, crisp
by crisp. There was a lot of noisy scrunching and
then a loud smacking of lips as it went nosing
about the rocks to make sure it hadn't missed one.

As he watched its fumbling movements, Richie realized with surprise that the little green eyes couldn't see very far, and the fact that his visitor was shortsighted as well as slow made it even less alarming.

When it was satisfied that there was nothing left on the rocks, it lifted its head to the level of Richie's hands and waited patiently, peering expectantly toward the half-empty bag.

"Ah, you're awful nice!" cried Richie with a little laugh. Suddenly he wanted to feed it properly, out of his hand, as he would feed a horse with an apple. So he scooped out the rest of the crisps and held them out on his palm.

As the creature's face came closer, he felt its breath on his fingers, not warm and smelling of hay like the breath of a horse, but cool, with a tang of seaweed, reminding him of the air in a damp sea cave. A couple of crisps blew away in the draft, but the creature stooped and sucked them up and then came back for the rest, seeming to hold its breath as it reached out toward Richie's hand. Then out flicked an ice-cold tongue and the whole pile disappeared, sucked out of sight with that *shlooooooop* he had heard before.

The head continued to hover in front of Richie, the eyes watching him hopefully.

"I'm afraid I haven't got any more," he said, turning the empty bag upside down to prove his words. But the creature flicked out its tongue again, and before Richie could do a thing it had swallowed the bag as well!

"Oh, I say, that might give you a pain, you know!" Richie warned, eyeing the great beast anxiously.

Now that he was close to it, he saw that it was not so rock-colored as he had thought. The head and neck gleamed with deep shades of green and indigo and purple, while the same colors were repeated in even deeper tones on as much of the body as could be seen above the water. And yet there were light tones too, reflecting the water in which it lay.

"I suppose that's what makes him so hard to spot, between the sea and the rocks," decided Richie.

And then as before he heard that puzzling extra *CLONG* mixed up with the sound of the bell buoy. And once again the creature began to move away, heading slowly out to sea in a confusing swirl of foam, until it was impossible to tell which of the dark wet humps in the sea were rocks and which were not.

But this time Richie felt happier. Not only had the beast come back, it had actually eaten out of his hand. He now felt very hopeful that it would return again.

It did return again . . . and again . . . and yet again. Then there was a gap of several days, and just as he was getting really worried, it came smiling in from the sea once more.

It was the start of a strange, secret friendship. Richie sometimes wondered why he wasn't afraid of such an enormous creature, and when he thought about it in bed at night, he shivered under the bedclothes. However, he soon discovered that his new friend's brain was as slow as its lumbering movements, and who could be afraid of anything so gentle and dim-witted?

As the days went by, Richie began to realize that the creature's arrival depended not only on the potato crisps but also on the tides. He noticed that it only appeared when the water was high enough to allow it to come right into the secret bay, within reach of the cliffside flowers and grass on which it liked to graze.

"So that explains the uprooted grass," said Richie to himself.

He began to study his new friend's tastes and found that it liked apples and tomatoes as well as crisps. It did not care for bread or biscuits and turned away from a hard-boiled egg, but reached out eagerly for gooseberries, and even cherries, which it swallowed stones and all. It was soon clear that this strange creature from the sea would eat anything that grew, tearing at leaves and cliff-side plants wherever these came within reach of its outstretched neck.

Now that Richie knew what it liked to eat, he began collecting food for it. He picked up a battered basket on the tide line, and into this he gathered leaves and fruit and any other delicacies he could find, so that when the creature came

nosing into the secret bay it would find him waiting on the rocks with a basketful of greenstuff as
well as a bag of potato crisps.

In time it dawned on Richie that somebody
must be watching over his new friend because
every day as the tide began to ebb, and before
the water became shallow enough to strand the
enormous creature on the shore, there came that
curious extra bell note, calling it away. And although the sleepy beast was sometimes slow to
respond, it always obeyed in the end, pausing
only long enough to snatch one last mouthful
before moving out into deeper water, where it
was quickly lost to sight among the rocks.

*Chapter Four*

It was Richie's favorite kind of day, warm and still and magical, the sunlight softened by a dreamlike haze and the sea like shining glass. The tide was almost high as he scrambled up to his lookout post to watch for the arrival of his friend.

"Only the funny thing is I never see him coming," he mused. "One minute the sea is full of rocks, and the next minute one of them isn't a rock at all!" Even while he was thinking this, it happened again and there was the nice old foolish face blinking up from the sea below.

He knew now that sudden movements did not worry this strange creature, so with a whoop of welcome he slid down from his perch and ran out across the flat rocks to where the comical face was rearing up out of the sea.

"Yes, I've brought you lots of treats today," he called. "Steady on, though. Don't shove me over!"

And he stepped back, laughing, as the huge creature buried its nose in the basket, snuffling with
pleasure. It was an untidy feeder, and the rocks
were soon littered with leaves and trails of honey-
suckle. But when the basket was empty the long
neck bent over the rocks and the scattered fragments were slowly sucked up in their turn.

"Just like a big vacuum cleaner!" chuckled
Richie to himself.

But the visitor did not only come for food.
When it had finished eating, it lay about in the
water, letting the little waves wash over its back
and watching Richie lazily as though it liked his
company.

Presently, as the waves slapped higher around
its sides, it humped its great back out of the water
and began to scratch itself, rubbing up and down
against a jutting ledge of rock.

"Here, let me help!" cried Richie, jumping forward. But his fingers made no impression and the
creature went on rubbing against the ledge, quite
unaware of Richie's puny efforts.

"I must look for something scratchier," decided
Richie. He wandered off and searched in the

nearby rock pools until he found a stout old oyster shell, rough with ancient barnacles. This was exactly what was needed, and as he got to work with it, he felt the beast's whole body relax as it gave itself up to this pleasurable new sensation.

Before long, it humped a new area of its back up out of the water to come within reach of the scratching shell—or almost within reach.

"Come a bit closer, can you?" called Richie, standing on tiptoe as he tried to reach the spot with his shell. But he stretched a little too far, and his feet slipped on the wet rock. At the same moment a wave surged up around his ankles, almost sweeping him off his feet. He made a wild grab, and as a second wave came swirling in he managed to hoist himself up beyond its reach.

It was only now that Richie discovered that he

had not climbed up on a rock as he supposed. He had hoisted himself on to the ridge of the great beast's back!

He drew in a frightened breath and held it, trying to make himself as light as air as he waited to see what would happen next. Animals may enjoy being petted and fed, but lots of them don't like people scrambling on to their backs!

But the great beast hadn't even noticed he was there. Its whole attention was on something else. And then Richie heard it too: *clang-clung-CLONG* . . . *clang-clung-CLONG* . . .

He felt no movement, but when he looked down he saw that already a stretch of water lay between himself and the rock on which he had been standing. Now he was really frightened.

"Wait! Wait! Let me get down before you go!" he shrilled, thumping the horny back with his fists and drumming his heels against the rock-hard sides.

Nothing happened except that the stretch of water widened. The beast's slow brain could only deal with one idea at a time, and at the moment that one idea was to keep heading out to sea.

Richie leaned forward, beating on the back of the thick neck with all his strength, and shouted at the top of his voice, timing his words to come between the insistent calls of the bell note. And then at last the head half turned in his direction.

"Please, will you take me back to the shore before you go away?" he implored again.

He felt a quiver run through the heavy body, as though the bewildered creature was uncertain whether to obey the call of the bell or the pleading voice in its ear. But the call of the bell proved stronger, and to Richie's dismay, there was no turning back. Yet at the same time there was a comforting glint in the little green eye as it rolled in his direction, and he suddenly felt confident that this huge lumbering animal really was his friend.

"And surely a friend as big as this will make everything all right," he thought. His spirits began to rise, and unclenching his fists, he settled down on the great beast's back and looked about him. Gradually it dawned on him that this was what he had wanted all his life.

This was going to be a real adventure!

*Chapter Five*

Drifting with the ebbing tide, they moved out among the little islands that Richie had studied so longingly from the shore. There were even more than he had guessed, and many that seemed no more than barren rocks were tufted with flowers and waving grasses. They neared the rock where the cormorants stood holding out their great dark wings to dry, and he now saw nests and fledgling chicks on the rock behind them. As

for the larger skerries, they were just the size that islands ought to be, with the sea in sight on every side whichever way one looked. And this was the perfect way to see them, since the great beast drifted closer to the island shores than any boat would dare.

Richie was so busy looking at everything they passed that he paid no attention to the sea itself until a sudden wave slapped up, drenching him with spray. He looked around then and was startled to see breaking crests on every side and the bell buoy rolling among them. He wondered why the glass-calm sea had suddenly grown so rough, and then, with a tingle of fear, he realized

what had happened. They had left the tranquil water behind and moved out into the tide rip he had seen from the window. Mrs. Moffatt's words came back to him now: "No boat ever built could stay right side up in that."

But the creature he was riding was bigger than any small boat, and there was something safe and comforting in the placid way it plowed steadily through the angry waves as though they were not there.

"Besides," said Richie to himself, "he's my friend and this is our adventure."

They passed quite close to the bell buoy and Richie was surprised to discover how large it was. The sound of its bell was deafening at close quarters. But he noticed at once that it tolled only the two familiar notes: *clang-clung* . . . *clang-clung* . . . And then he heard a faint *CLONG* . . . *CLONG* . . . coming over the sea like an echo.

"Perhaps there's another buoy out there somewhere," he thought, trying to peer ahead. But he could see nothing beyond the haze of fine spray that hung over the tide rip like a mist. He tried to look back but the shore was also lost in haze and already seemed less real than this enchanted voyage among the little islands.

Gradually the bell buoy slid astern and they forged through the frothing tidal channel into calm water beyond. As they sailed clear of the tide-rip haze, Richie glanced ahead once more, and there was the great mass of Muckle Craig looming up so close and clear that he could see bright clumps of bluebells growing in the crevices of its rose-pink rocks and hear the cries of sea birds wheeling over it.

The Craig was very much larger than could be guessed from the shore, its grassy crest rising up in a towering peak at the seaward end. Below this peak the cliff fell away in a sheer, breath-taking precipice to the sea. As the beast swam slowly around the base of the cliff, Richie stared up in awe, imagining how it would look on a stormy day with wild breakers flinging their spray high against that sheer pink wall of rock.

Then the full sweep of the precipice came into view and he saw that the lower half was gashed by the entrance to a vast, dark cavern, where the sea sucked slowly in and out, in and out, with quiet gurgling sounds. He leaned forward, trying to peer into the dark interior and thinking how exciting it would be to go inside and explore.

But when the creature he was riding slowly altered course and headed in toward the opening, Richie was suddenly not so sure. His knees gripped the rock-hard sides and he whispered apprehensively: "Shall we . . . shall we wait till another day, perhaps?"

The creature gave no sign that it heard or understood, continuing to move steadily in toward the cliff until, with startling suddenness, the hazy sunshine was abruptly blotted out and they were inside the shadowed cavern, with the sharp tang of seaweed all about them.

The still air was icy cold and Richie shivered as he strained his eyes in the darkness. But he could see little beyond the black water rippling away on either side, to break in a dim line of pale foam against unseen walls of rock. The sound of these little splashes was magnified into a continuous watery murmur that echoed around the invisible roof overhead, until Richie began to feel that they were submerged in water that he could neither see nor feel.

But if Richie could not see the way, the great beast clearly knew where it was going and glided forward steadily. Then out of the darkness boomed the *CLONG . . . CLONG . . .* of the deep-toned bell, and as the quivering sound reverberated around the hidden cavern walls, it seemed to Richie to be calling *"Come . . . come . . ."*

A glimmer of light appeared ahead and he wondered if they were about to come out on the far side of the Craig. But he soon saw that the light was pouring in through a crevice in the wall that looked like an odd-shaped window, framed in leaves and ferns. Outside this opening, silhouetted against the sunlit sea, hung a roughly made rope ladder. As Richie gaped in astonishment, it began to quiver, and presently a pair of bare feet came into view, climbing down the ladder, rung by rung from above.

*Chapter Six*

Richie watched, more curious than scared, as a pair of legs in rolled-up jeans came slowly down the ladder. The jeans were old and shabby, and the legs short and bent and very brown. Next a tattered fisherman's jersey came into view, and finally a sturdy little figure dropped to the ground and came toward the opening with the rolling gait of a sailor. His features were indistinct against the sunlit sky, but Richie saw a fringe of grizzled beard around his chin and a knitted cap pulled down over sparse white hair. In one hand he carried a bulging sack.

He stood for a moment in the opening, stooping forward as his eyes tried to penetrate the gloom. Then in a deep, husky voice he called out something that sounded like: "Atoo ungo?"

"Oh, he speaks a different language," Richie thought despondently.

But the strange-sounding words had an immediate effect on the great beast, which began to wallow from side to side in the water, sending waves rippling away in all directions, to slap and echo eerily in the hidden depths of the cavern.

This performance seemed to be all the reply the little stranger expected, for he stepped straight in out of the sunshine and clambered down a flight of rough steps cut in the rock below the opening. As soon as he reached the water's edge, he began to untie his sack and Richie saw that it was full of greenstuff. The beast was clearly expecting this, and before the sack was fully opened, it surged forward and thrust its head inside. The little man laughed and spoke in an affectionate,

teasing tone. Richie made no attempt to understand, until he was startled to hear quite plainly: ". . . all the time in the world to eat it, old fellow."

So it wasn't a foreign language after all, simply a different way of pronouncing the one he knew, just as he and the Scottish children so often said the same words differently.

However, in spite of having all the time in the world, the beast quickly emptied the sack and then stooped its long neck to suck up a few scattered leaves from the black surface of the water. In the same moment the little man glanced up and caught sight of Richie perched high on the humped back in the shadows. His mouth fell open and for a moment he gaped as though he simply could not believe what he saw. Then he froze back against the steps like a wild animal that hopes it won't be noticed if it keeps as still as a rock.

There was a long quivering silence, broken at last by the husky voice demanding in little more than a whisper: "Whatever have you brought in, Mungo?"

The words were oddly pronounced, but Richie found he could understand perfectly well if he put his mind to it, and he listened carefully to the next anxiously muttered question: "Why did you bring him in here to our secret place, you silly old thing?"

The great beast made no reply, merely hanging its head as though embarrassed, and although Richie could not see its face, he could picture its foolish, apologetic smile. Feeling suddenly sorry for his gentle, slow-witted friend, he sat up very straight and spoke out boldly in its defense.

"It wasn't his fault, really it wasn't. I was helping to scratch his back when he suddenly heard that special bell and began swimming out to sea like he always does when he hears it. He didn't even feel me on his back, and by the time I made him understand, it was too late."

"Ah, it would be, it always is too late with Mungo," agreed the little stranger with a sigh. "He's slow, awful slow, that's his trouble."

"But that's one of the things I like about him," Richie said quickly. "Anything as big as this and clever too would be pretty frightening, don't you think?" And he leaned down to stroke the smooth curve of the drooping neck.

A long silence followed and Richie was beginning to hope he hadn't annoyed the little stranger when the queer deep voice said unexpectedly: "You'll want to pat him harder than that if he's to feel you. His skin is as hard as rock." Then, looking searchingly up at Richie, he went on, "Seems as though you like old Mungo."

"Oh, yes, I do, terrifically," cried Richie. "I watch out for him every day."

"Watch out for him? Why? Are you trying to catch him?"

"Catch him? However could I?" gasped Richie. "Anyway, seems more like he's caught me!"

At that, the little man laughed suddenly, and the beast, sensing that he was no longer in disgrace, showed his delight by plunging and rolling in the water, until great waves splashed up around his sides, all but sweeping Richie off his perch.

"That's how he is when he's pleased," the little man explained. "You'd better come down off him now before he has the waves washing you off in his excitement. He forgets how big he is. Whisht now, Mungo, move over here to the steps and keep still while the lad gets down."

The beast edged obediently across to where the little man reached out a hand to guide Richie down to the bottom step with the warning: "Careful now, it's awful slippery after all his lashing about."

"And now let's have a proper look at you," he went on, keeping a firm grip on Richie's hand as he pulled him up the steps and out into the open.

Richie blinked in the strong light, dazzled after the gloom of the cavern. He was aware at once of the scent of flowers, and when he opened his eyes, he found himself in a natural rock garden where sea pinks, sea lavender, and great drifts of white sea campion spread over wide steps of rose-pink rock, while thyme and yellow rock roses cascaded down from ledge to ledge in waterfalls of color.

He sat down on a sun-warmed slab of rock and stared about him. The garden stretched as far along the cliff as he could see, and as high as a ledge over which the rope ladder disappeared from view, far up on the glowing cliff face.

When he turned back to his companion, he found the little man studying him in silence. Having had a good look at one side, he walked slowly around to the other, still saying nothing. Richie was reminded of the way strange dogs meet and inspect one another, and he wondered suddenly if perhaps the little fellow rarely saw another human being.

The silence was broken at last by an abrupt statement, proudly spoken: "I'm Skipper." The old blue eyes watched Richie keenly, as though wondering what impression this announcement would make. When his news was received with no more than a casual nod, he tweaked his knitted cap to a jauntier angle and went on grandly, "They used to call me Boy, but I'm Skipper now! What's your name?"

"Richie."

"H'm, sounds all right. And you look all right, bit on the small and skinny side, but I was small myself as a lad."

"And still pretty small!" thought Richie with a private twitch of amusement.

The little fellow now came closer and Richie

was surprised by the worried expression in his wrinkled face as he asked imploringly, "You won't tell about Mungo, will you?"

"Not tell?" said Richie, very much surprised. It's true he hadn't told anyone yet, but only because he hadn't met anyone who would believe his story. "Why mustn't I tell?"

"Because if people heard he was here they'd come out with nets and traps and capture him and put him in a zoo, I know they would. Just imagine poor old Mungo cooped up in a concrete pool for everyone to stare at, and no deep, shady place to hide in, and nobody to scratch his back or anything. And the trouble is he's so slow and simple he'd let them catch him easy."

There was a quiver in the husky voice as the old fellow begged again, "Promise you won't tell anyone? Promise?"

"All right, I won't tell," agreed Richie and was rewarded with a beaming, gap-toothed smile. Now it was his turn to ask a question: "What exactly is Mungo? I mean, what kind of an animal is he?"

"He's one of the last—perhaps by this time quite the last—of the old sea monsters."

"A . . . *monster?* You mean like the Loch Ness Monster?"

"Don't know, never heard of the Loch Ness Monster."

"Never heard of it?" Richie was astounded.

"Well and how would I hear of it? I don't never see folks close enough to talk to, even if I do watch them through my telescope. And I don't let Mungo go near people either if I can help it. That's why I've taught him to come when I ring the bell."

"So it's you!" interrupted Richie.

"Aye," said Skipper, "I ring that bell so I can call him back before he gets stranded by the tide, or takes a fancy to go inland up some creek or sea loch. He's so foolish he'd try anything. I thought he was safe enough on this deserted coast since nobody ever goes boating here. They all seem to go climbing in these parts. Beats me, though, how I never spotted you."

"I try not to be spotted," admitted Richie in a small voice. Then a new thought struck him and he asked, "Is there anyone else on Muckle Craig besides you and Mungo?"

Skipper shook his head and Richie went on with

a puzzled frown, "How did you get here, then? Mrs. Moffatt says nobody ever comes out here. Did Mungo bring you too?"

"Och no, Mungo was here years before I came, a hundred years or more for all I know. I've no idea where he came from or how long he'd been in there in that old pool. Most of his sort died out long ago because they weren't bright enough to keep up with cleverer animals in a changing world."

"Poor things," murmured Richie softly. "How do you suppose Mungo managed then, since he's so big and slow?"

"Well, of course his slowness is a help in one way because he just looks like part of the scenery when he goes out among all those rocks. And then he's not all that big—"

"Not big?" interrupted Richie in astonishment.

"Not really. Monsters of his sort used to be three or four times his size. And then of course he's been lucky in his choice of a home. Nowhere could be much safer than Muckle Craig with the tide rip keeping everyone away. And look, here he comes to join us now!" Skipper went on, laughing as Mungo's comical face appeared at the rocky window.

"But surely he's too big to get out through that little opening?" said Richie doubtfully.

"Oh, he doesn't want to come right out, he'd much rather lie in the cool water down below. But at the same time he likes to poke his head out for company." And Skipper held out a welcoming hand as the smooth head on its long neck came snaking out of the hole and over the rocks to where they sat among the flowers.

"So you've come out to join us, have you?" said Skipper as the head came to rest on his knee. "All right, I know, you want to be tickled under the chin!" He chuckled as the green eyes looked up beseechingly.

"I'll help too," said Richie, moving across so that he could rub his fingers along the opposite side of the smooth jaw.

"Funny when you come to think of it," Skipper went on musingly. "There was I setting out from Scotland as a youngster to see the world and all its wonders, and what should I do but find the biggest wonder of them all right here at home in Scotland, eh, Mungo?"

He fell silent, absently fondling Mungo's head until the great beast closed his eyes contentedly. Richie began to fear that Skipper might also drop asleep if he didn't prod him with another question.

"How did you get here then, if Mungo didn't bring you?" he asked.

"I was shipwrecked here," said Skipper simply.

Chapter Seven

"Tell me about being shipwrecked," begged Richie eagerly, his eyes on Skipper's face. "I've never met a real live castaway."

"It was all a long, long while ago," mused Skipper reminiscently. "I was a lad about your size, though a few years older than you'd be now, when I joined the *Bonnie Bluebell*. And bonny she was in my eyes on the proud day when I signed on as ship's boy. That's why they called me Boy, like I told you."

Richie nodded silently and Skipper went on: "Second night out it was, when we ran into a proper old gale, and before we rightly knew it, we were on the rocks and nothing we could do to save ourselves. I never saw such a storm before or since. I'll never forget the way those great waves went on a-battering and a-pounding all night long until poor old *Bluebell* was broke clean in two.

"Well, I reckon I was the lucky one that night, since I was trapped in the little galley where I'd gone to brew a mug of tea for the skipper. All on my own I was, and I can tell you I was terrified, what with the screeching of the wind and the thumping of the ship and the awful creakings of the galley walls round me."

Richie let out his pent-up breath in a long shuddering sigh as Skipper went on: "Anyway, when daylight came, I found myself on the rocks here, with my shipmates gone and no more than the battered shell of the galley round me. The rest of the ship was smashed to splinters. Fortunately the tide was low and I'd just wits enough left to drag myself up to the rocks above high water."

"And then?" breathed Richie as Skipper lapsed into silence, his eyes fixed unseeingly on the far horizon.

"Well, for a while I reckon I just lay there, hoping someone would come and rescue me. But nobody came and I began to feel hungry, so I sat up and looked about me.

"At first it didn't look too bad. The sun was shining after the storm and the sky was blue and the seagulls wheeling round. I got to me feet and climbed higher up the cliff there, and then it suddenly dawned on me that I'd fetched up on Muckle Craig. I'd heard about the Craig, of course, and I knew that sailors took good care to keep clear of it. So I knew very well that no boat would ever come close enough to see me. I'd nothing to make signals with, and even when I'd learned to make a fire by rubbing sticks together I realized that nobody would see the smoke on account of the mist of spray that the tide rip spreads round the Craig."

Richie became aware of a movement as Mungo shifted his position and opened a reproachful green eye.

"Sorry, old friend, was I forgetting to tickle you

then?" mumbled Skipper apologetically, and his fingers went to work again as he went on: "So I soon realized there was nothing for it but to set about discovering what sort of a living the old Craig would provide for me. And indeed it wasn't too bad at all. There's a couple of good clear springs that never dry up, and plenty to eat, once you've made up your mind you've got to make do with shellfish and seaweeds and such. Of course there's other fish too, when you can catch them, and sea-gulls' eggs in season. And later I found watercress and blaeberries up above on the Craig."

"What about *Bluebell*?" questioned Richie. "Were there any stores left in the galley?"

"A few odds and ends were washed up on the rocks, but they were mostly ruined by salt water. Other things came ashore too in time—the ship's bell bolted to a great piece of timber, and part of a locker with the ship's papers. It was when those papers came ashore that I realized it was all mine now, and since there was nobody to contradict me I called myself 'Mate.' It was a step up from ship's boy, and even though there was nobody to impress I was mighty pleased with myself, I can tell you."

The one who was not impressed was Mungo, who now opened both eyes in a mute reminder that grand-sounding titles did nothing to get a fellow properly tickled under the chin.

"My fingers keep forgetting," apologized Skipper, bending to the task once more. With a contented sigh, the creature closed his eyes again, and Skipper took up his tale.

"It must have been a couple of years later, when I was picking over driftwood in a cave, that I came on the skipper's sea chest with his best hat and his telescope. I was scared to touch his things at first. He'd been a hard man, our captain. But in time I came to accept the fact that he was gone with the rest. And even supposing any of them had managed to get to the mainland shore that night, they'd never come out here to Muckle Craig, that was very certain. And so, since I was the only member of the crew remaining with the wreckage of the *Bonnie Bluebell,* then surely I was skipper of what was left of the poor old ship? So that's how I came to take on the name of Skipper, see?" There was a wistful note in the husky voice as he added: "Not that there's much point in being skipper when there's nobody left to say 'Aye, aye, sir.' Old Mungo here would never understand things like that, even if he could talk. Just look at him now, he's dropped asleep while I've been speaking!"

"And you mean you actually live here all the time on Muckle Craig?" asked Richie. When the little fellow nodded, he persisted: "But what about winter? How do you keep warm? And where do you get clothes and things?" He eyed the knitted cap, which looked almost new.

"I'll show you," said Skipper. He slid neatly from under Mungo's sleeping head, which he lowered gently on to a cushion of purple thyme without disturbing the great beast. Then, signing to Richie to follow, he led the way to the foot of the rope ladder, calling back over his shoulder as he went: "This way, follow me."

"Aye, aye, sir!" answered Richie.

Skipper made no reply, he did not even turn his head, but there was a new jauntiness about his back as he started up the ladder.

*Chapter Eight*

Richie had never climbed a rope ladder before and this was the longest he had ever seen, going up and up and up to a wide shelf of rock high on the face of the towering pink cliff. But Skipper was already scrambling up, so there was nothing to do but follow, clinging to the swaying ropes and struggling up from rung to rung as best he could. At times the ladder swung so close to the cliff that he thought he must graze his knees and knuckles, and he shut his eyes, waiting for the crash. Then a crowd of clamoring sea birds appeared, wheeling round and round until he felt quite dizzy. Skipper swung around once to yell at them: "Och, will ye hush? I'm not wanting your eggs today."

But his words made no impression on the birds and the uproar only died away when he reached the top of the ladder and scrambled on to the ledge, leaning back to catch Richie firmly by the arm and haul him up beside him.

Richie looked about him curiously. They were
standing on a wide platform of jutting rock running half way across the cliff face. The first thing
that caught his eye was a brass ship's bell hanging
from a stout iron bar driven into the rock wall. A
length of rope hung from the heavy clapper, and

around the outside of the bell he saw letters engraved in the metal. Stepping closer, he spelled out *Bonnie Bluebell.*

"The bell from the wreck," he murmured, running his fingers over the lettering. "Is this the one you ring for Mungo?"

"Aye, that's the one. But come along and see the rest."

As Richie turned to follow, he saw at once that this was no ordinary ledge. Although so high above the sea, it was heaped with driftwood, neatly stacked against the cliff, together with every sort of object ever washed in by the tide. There were great heaps of fishing nets and coils of rope, glass balls and aluminum floats, electric lightbulbs and odd, misshapen candles, and toys and balls and corks and plastic objects of every sort and color.

And then he saw the most intriguing thing of all. At the back of the ledge, built up against the cliff, was an enchanting little house entirely made of driftwood and other odds and ends from the tide line. The walls were made of planks, tree trunks, and wooden hatch covers, cleverly fastened together with nails and knotted rope. Here and there ships' portholes and other odd-shaped windows peeped out through a patchwork of overlapping boards, the crevices plugged with long-dried clay. The roof was thickly thatched with dried seaweed held in place by lengths of rope weighed down with heavy boulders. There was even a cock-eyed chimney made from a length of cracked piping secured with twisted wire.

As Richie stood and stared at the astonishing little building, Skipper watched him with a happy smile.

"My home, I hope you like it," he said simply.
"Come inside." And he pushed open a massive
door heavily studded with nails.

"Wait, I haven't seen all the outside yet," cried Richie, pausing to examine a window shutter labeled *Outspan Oranges.*

"Plenty of time to go over it all again later," called Skipper. "Besides, it's just as good inside as out, come on in and see for yourself."

"Aye, aye, sir," said Richie, following him indoors.

The door opened into a comfortable room with boarded walls and a hodgepodge of interesting furniture. Most of the chairs had odd legs cut down to size, and the table had three plain legs and one fat curly one ending in a carved claw foot. There was even a home-made desk, its cubbyholes crammed with pens and pencils from the tide line.

The walls were hung with shells, dried starfish, and delicate sprays of white coral. There were even wrinkled pictures torn from tattered magazines and comics, held in place by rusted nails. One side of the room was filled with tools ranged in home-made racks along the wooden wall. The tools were mostly home-made too. There were heavy objects evidently used as makeshift hammers, and pieces of metal, nails, and bones had been twisted, sharpened, chipped, and filed into chisels and hooks and bradawls.

"Did you build this whole house yourself with all these tools?" asked Richie.

"Aye," nodded Skipper. "Built it bit by bit over the years with whatever the tide brought in. Come along and see the rest."

The house turned out to be larger than it appeared from the outside because the cliff against which it had been built was honeycombed with little caves that opened out at the back of the house, forming extra rooms. These were cooler than those in the wooden house and were chiefly used as storerooms. One made a little washroom with running water dripping down over the rocks at the back, to seep away through a crack in the stone floor. A shelf of rock along one wall was stacked with sponges. Brightly colored polythene pails and basins stood about the floor.

"And now for my cabin," said Skipper. "Mind your head as you come up the companionway, that bulkhead's rather awkward."

Richie was mystified by these strange nautical terms, but when they reached the tiny attic bedroom he saw at once that it really was like a ship's cabin with its bunk bed and round porthole. An upturned barrel served as a bedside table and on it stood a lopsided candle stuck in an empty bottle. Above the bed, an officer's peaked cap hung from a rusty nail.

"Captain's," said Skipper briefly, lifting it down and fingering its tarnished gold.

"The one that came out of the sea chest?" asked Richie.

"Aye. And although I called myself Skipper, it was years and years before I dared wear this. But when my hair began to turn white I reckoned that even supposing the old man was still alive, he'd be on the retired list now and not in need of this." With which he clapped the cap on his head and swung around proudly to let Richie see the full effect.

Richie whistled, very much impressed. Then, remembering where he was, he clicked his bare heels together and drew himself up with a splendid salute.

Skipper tried to look as though he was used to

this sort of thing as he took off the cap and hung it back on its nail.

"Of course I don't wear it every day," was all he said. But although he spoke in a casual tone Richie could see by his heightened color that he was secretly delighted.

"And here's the rest of my wardrobe," he went on, pulling back a sliding door. Behind it hung an astonishing collection of garments, men's, women's, and children's, together with dozens of caps and beach hats in all the colors of the rainbow. Underneath stood a long row of boots and shoes and sandshoes, mostly odd, but arranged as nearly as possible in matching styles and sizes.

"All brought in by the tide," he explained. "The sea brings me everything I have, it's my shop and parcel post and everything—I'll show you."

Once again Richie hung back, eyeing a handsome sea chest and longing for time to examine the folding chair. But Skipper was so thrilled to have a visitor that he wanted to show him everything at once, and was already on his way toward the rope ladder.

*Chapter Nine*

They found Mungo still asleep, with his head cushioned on the scented mound of wild thyme. Richie crept past on tiptoe so as not to disturb him, but Skipper called laughingly over his shoulder: "No need to be so careful, you'll not wake old Mungo once he's really off." And to prove his words he gave the beast an affectionate slap in passing. Mungo went on sleeping without so much as a twitch.

Skipper now turned his back on the cavern and made his way to the far end of the rock garden, where the lower part of the cliff jutted out to form a rocky promontory, hiding what lay beyond. Suddenly he stooped and plunged into a low cave in the base of the promontory.

"This way, follow me," he called as he vanished into the shadows.

"Aye . . . aye, sir," faltered Richie, groping after him.

"This is no more than a tunnel through the promontory. We'll soon be out the other side." Skipper's voice came back reassuringly out of the darkness, and almost as he spoke, a twist in the passage brought them within sight and sound of the sea. A few more shuffling paces and they were out in the open.

The passage led to a small cove under the cliff, but any sand or rocks there may have been were completely hidden under the biggest mass of drift-wood Richie had even seen.

"I just didn't know there could be so much, all washed in in one place," he marveled, staring around. There were huge balks of bleached timber, uprooted trees, and a jumbled mass of wreckage, all piled up in wild confusion, just as the tides had swept them in year after year after year. Richie scrambled to the highest point he could reach, on the roof of a wrecked beach hut carried in on a spring tide long ago and now half submerged under more recent flotsam. He stood on the tilted roof and stared about in silence.

"This is where I came in with the wreck of the poor old *Bluebell*," remarked Skipper. "Everything gets washed in here. Must be something to do with the set of the tide rip, I suppose. You never know what the sea will bring in next, that's what makes it so exciting."

"I see what you mean about it being like a sort of shop and parcel post all in one," said Richie, disentangling a battered kettle from a heap of wet seaweed and frayed rope.

"Now you see why my house is never finished and never will be," went on Skipper. "Because I'm always finding something new to add to it. Look

at this now." And he held up half a window with panes of colored glass. "I've been longing to find a use for this for ages, so it's a good thing we'll be needing a new room now. Oh, and here's something new since I was last here." And he stooped to examine a long board glittering with dried salt crystals. The underside was still damp when he turned it over.

Suddenly he straightened up and looked at Richie speculatively, then surprised him with a question: "How strong are you? You don't look all that tough, but no more did I at your age. We little ones are often stronger than we appear."

"Oh yes, I'm as strong as strong," Richie assured him quickly, squaring his shoulders and clenching his fists to prove his strength.

"Fine. Then maybe you'll help me get some of these long pieces up. They're awkward to move alone." And he waved a hand toward a number of heavy planks upended against the cliff at the back of the cove.

"It'll be grand to have a chance to use this lot," he went on happily. "So now, you wait here, will you, while I go up and fix a rope to the winch.

Then I'll come back and show you what to do."
And away he hurried through the tunnel, to reappear five minutes later swarming up the ladder where it came into view above the promontory.

Left to himself, Richie rummaged contentedly. He liked nothing better than poking about among the driftwood left by the tides, and his pockets were always crammed with treasures picked up along the shore. But this was something beyond his wildest dreams.

"Like a sort of Aladdin's cave, only this kind of treasure is much more fun than gold and jewels," he decided, dragging a fine green shrimping net from under a jumbled mass of branches and dried kelp.

He was interrupted by a shout from above and looked up to see Skipper peering down from the ledge on the cliff face far above. Then he began to lower a rope over the edge.

"Call out when it reaches you and then allow a few more feet for tying," Skipper shouted, paying out the rope at such a speed that it came writhing down like a snake. When its free end swung within reach, Richie grabbed it, hitched several loops

around his arm, and then called up, holding out the coil for inspection.

Skipper waved and nodded, and soon came hurrying down to join him. He showed Richie which planks they would want for a start, and between them they carried the first of these to the foot of the cliff. Here Skipper lashed the end of the rope around it, securing it with a very impressive knot.

"Now," he said, straightening up, "I'll go up top and winch this up. Your job will be to hold it clear of the cliff as long as you can and make sure it's in the right position."

"And what if it isn't?" questioned Richie anxiously.

"Just give me a shout and I'll stop hauling and slack away till we get it right," said Skipper. "As to the window, I'd better carry that up myself, its glass might get broken against the cliff if we haul it up on the rope." He picked up the window, edged it sideways into the tunnel, and was soon creeping carefully up the ladder with his awkward burden.

Richie had never before been trusted with such a responsible job, and he clenched his teeth as the first heavy plank began to move. It was an unwieldy load to hold clear of the cliff, but he managed it somehow, standing on tiptoe until it was beyond his reach. Then he watched it swing slowly up the cliff until it reached the ledge, where Skipper hauled it over the top and out of sight.

In this way they raised five large planks. Then, instead of lowering the rope again, Skipper called from above: "All right, that's enough to be going on with for the moment. Come along up now and we'll get started."

"Good-O!" shouted Richie, dropping a couple of boards with a crash as he scrambled across the piled driftwood and darted into the tunnel.

*Chapter Ten*

Half way up the ladder, Richie stopped so suddenly that the lower rungs swung against the cliff
with a clatter that scattered the screaming gulls in
all directions. But he had something more impor-
tant to think about than seagulls. For the first time
since the day's adventure started, he was remembering the time.

He glanced hastily out to sea. The steamer was
not in sight. However, he knew she must soon be
on her way, and there was a sinking feeling in his
heart as he climbed to the top of the ladder and
hoisted himself on to the rock shelf.

Then, swallowing hard, he forced himself to say:
"I want to help with the building more than anything in the world. But I'm afraid I'll have to go
home quite soon."

"*Go home?*" echoed Skipper in dismay. "Just
when we're going to build a special room for you!"

"A room . . . for *me?*" stammered Richie.

"Of course it's for you. Why else would I want an extra room?" said Skipper, quite forgetting that he had already told Richie that his house was never finished and never would be.

"Anyway, why should you want to go away when Mungo's brought you here?"

"Well, there's Aunt Hilda, you see. She and I belong together," Richie explained.

Skipper said nothing, and Richie added lamely: "She'd worry if I was late."

Skipper still said nothing, and Richie went on desperately: "You see, I have to go back when the steamer passes, the one with the yellow fun—"

"I might have guessed it!" interrupted Skipper with a sigh. "It was just the same with Angus."

"Angus!" exclaimed Richie. "Do you know Angus? Does he come out here to Muckle Craig?"

"He used to come years ago. Mungo brought him out, same as he brought you."

"That's funny," mused Richie with a puzzled frown, "because Angus's mother was the person who told me that nobody ever comes out to Muckle Craig."

"Ah, but she wouldn't know about Mungo, you

see. Angus promised not to tell, same as you have promised. And except for Mungo, there isn't any other way to come."

"Was Angus a boy when he came to the Craig?" asked Richie.

"Aye, he was, although he was a good bit older than you, and he soon grew up and went away to a job. All the same, he really picked that job because he was so keen on Mungo. He was always scared in case some ship might go off course and land out here on the Craig and discover the monster and carry him off to a zoo, like I said before. And he knew, same as I do, that the poor silly old fellow would be easy caught. And then one day he came up that there ladder fair shouting with excitement. 'I know a way I can help keep Mungo safe!' he cried. 'I'm going to be a lighthouse keeper! That way I can help keep ships in their proper channels, well away from Muckle Craig and Mungo.' "

Suddenly Richie was on his feet, the past overshadowed by the immediate present.

"Look, oh look, here she comes!" he cried, pointing to a small dark speck on the horizon. He knew

it would not be long before that speck grew into the yellow-funneled steamer. There was no time to lose.

"Please, oh Skipper, please," he implored. "Will you ask Mungo to take me home again?"

"I can suggest it, but he won't like it, any more than I like it meself, after we've got you here and all," muttered Skipper dejectedly.

"Oh, Skipper, it isn't that I want to go," cried Richie. "But don't you see, I'll never be allowed to come out on my own again if I don't get home in time."

"Oh, I know," said Skipper grudgingly. "I'd worry too, of course, if Mungo didn't come home in time. Anyway, best go and see him, I suppose."

The great beast was still asleep, but the heavy-lidded eyes half opened as Skipper squatted down beside him and explained what Richie wanted him to do. At this, Mungo promptly shut his eyes again and settled back to sleep, pressing his head hard down into the cushion of thyme as though he never meant to leave it.

"I warned you he wouldn't like it and he doesn't," said Skipper helplessly. "And he's awful good at not understanding when he doesn't want to."

The steamer gave a distant toot and Richie swung around in desperation.

"Oh, Mungo, please!" he pleaded.

Mungo opened one green eye and rolled it questioningly toward him.

"*Please!*" repeated Richie very softly.

Mungo opened his other eye and after a long, considering stare he raised his head and withdrew it slowly into the cavern. Then they heard a sound of muffled splashing as the heavy body began to move in the water below.

"Quick, better seize your chance before he changes his mind," advised Skipper. They hurried into the cavern, where the beast lay ready and waiting, his great body humped against the bottom step.

"Good old fellow," smiled Skipper, rubbing his head affectionately.

"You will remind him to come back and fetch me over another day, won't you?" urged Richie as he climbed on to Mungo's back. "I've got to come back here, simply *got* to," he finished earnestly.

"I'll do my best," promised Skipper.

"Tomorrow?" pressed Richie. "I could ask Aunt Hilda to give me a picnic lunch so I could be over here all day."

"Could you catch the morning tide?"

"Oh yes, easily."

"Fine. And now you'd best be off."

But Richie hesitated. "Hadn't we better make quite sure that Mungo understands about tomorrow?" he asked anxiously.

"No use telling him yet," said Skipper. "He can only attend to one idea at a time. At the moment he's fixed on this idea of taking you home, so we mustn't get him muddled."

Richie realized he would have to be content with this, but he still had one more request to make. "You won't start building until I come, will you?"

"I won't," promised Skipper with a grin. "And now, Mungo, off you go, back to the mainland," he ordered clearly. As he spoke, he gave the great beast an affectionate slap which ended as a powerful shove to start him on his way.

There was a mighty swirl of churning water as Mungo circled ponderously around the cavern.

Then he turned and headed toward the outer entrance. The window opening dwindled to a mere pinprick of light behind them. Then a twist in the unseen waterway blotted it out and they moved on in total darkness.

Before long, Richie became aware of a curious rhythmical throb-throb-throbbing sound.

"It must be the steamer, but it sounds awfully close!" he muttered apprehensively, not realizing how much the sound was magnified by the water in the enclosed cavern. He leaned forward, drumming his heels impatiently against Mungo's unfeeling sides and wishing he had asked Skipper if there was any means of hurrying a slow-moving monster on its way.

They rounded another corner and the cavern entrance came into view. As they sailed out into the sunshine, Richie looked anxiously for the steamer. But although the throb of her engines had sounded so loud in the cavern, she was still some distance off.

As they moved out around the headland, Richie looked up, trying to pick out the high ledge with its driftwood house, but it was invisible from the water. Then a whirling commotion of gulls drew his attention to the top of the Craig, and there he spotted the tiny prancing figure of Skipper waving from the highest peak.

Richie's attention soon returned to the steamer and he was dismayed to see how far she had advanced since he left the cavern. He was so intent on watching her now that he had no time for anything else and never so much as noticed the bell buoy or the turbulent water of the tide rip as they passed through. He swung around anxiously to see how far they were from the shore, and there was the lookout rock looming close ahead.

"Oh, good old Mungo, you've done it!" he cried delightedly. "But however did you manage to come so fast? I never even felt you moving!"

The tide was too low for the secret bay, but they were able to come in close to the flat rocks below. As Richie slid from his high perch, Mungo stooped to tear at a tuft of crimsom seaweed. Almost at once the sound of the bell came echoing over the sea. Richie watched as the great beast turned obediently.

"Thank you, thank you, good old Mungo," he cried gratefully. "And you will come back for me again tomorrow, won't you?"

From the grassy cliff he turned to look back over the sea. There was nothing to be seen except rocks and tumbling waves. Which was just what he expected.

As he ran home along the clifftop track, he wondered just how long he had been away. It felt more like a week than an afternoon, and he thought uneasily that the steamer might have come and gone several times while he had been on Muckle Craig. But when he got in, Aunt Hilda turned from the stove with a smile.

"Ah, there's a good boy, I have your supper ready here," she said, stooping to open the oven door.

*Chapter Eleven*

Long before the tide was high next morning, Richie was up on his lookout rock, shading his eyes with both hands as he gazed steadily out to sea. He watched and watched and watched until his eyes began to water. When nothing appeared among the waves, he began to worry. Suppose Mungo had not understood after all? Or suppose he had simply refused to come over? He couldn't forget that obstinate face pressed firmly into the cushion of thyme! Or suppose—just suppose the whole adventure had been a dream?

Just as this thought became unbearable, a watery snuffle made him look down and there, right at the foot of his lookout post, was the familiar rocklike shape wallowing in the waves.

"Mungo! How could you have got there without my seeing you, when I've been watching every inch of the sea for every single minute?" he cried accusingly, slithering down to the edge of the wave-washed gully in which the great beast lay. Mungo merely licked his lips with a steel-blue tongue and rolled his eyes from the basket in Richie's right hand to the packet of crisps in his left.

"All right!" said Richie with a laugh. "Your treat first, then mine afterward. That's fair, isn't it?"

Mungo plunged his head into the basket and began to eat. When everything was finished and the scattered leaves had been sucked up from the rocks, Richie climbed on to the great beast's back, impatient to be off.

"Come on, Mungo, my turn now," he wheedled.

But Mungo had only just arrived and had no intention of going home in a hurry. So instead of heading out to sea as Richie hoped, he turned into the secret bay, where he half swam, half crawled ashore. His stumpy legs were scarcely strong enough to support his heavy body, so he went no farther than was necessary to reach the plants he wanted. And there Richie had to sit, waiting as patiently as he could while the long neck stretched out, swaying from side to side as the great beast tore at plants on the cliff.

At long last the bell sounded over the sea:
*CLONG . . . CLONG . . . CLONG . . .* Richie
wondered how he had ever confused it with the
bell buoy. Its note sounded quite distinct to him
now, just as it did to Mungo, who lumbered slowly
into the sea and started moving out into deeper
water.

Riding high on the monster's back, Richie found
it hard to believe that Mungo could ever be mis-
taken for a reef of rocks, and he glanced back
nervously, hoping they wouldn't be spotted from
the hotel as they made their way out to sea. He
might be able to persuade his aunt and Mrs.
Moffatt to keep the secret, but he could just
imagine Jeannie spreading the news like wildfire,
telling everyone she met that there was a real live
monster out on Muckle Craig. Before they came
in sight of the hotel, though, they were into the
foam at the fringe of the tide rip, where a cloud
of spray enfolded them, making them quite invisible from the shore.

Skipper was not on the high peak of the Craig
as they passed, and when they went into the

cavern they found him waiting at the foot of the steps with his sack.

"Oh, but Mungo's had simply heaps to eat already, really he has," cried Richie, fidgeting with impatience.

"Maybe he has, but there's an awful lot of him to feed, remember," said Skipper quietly. He opened the sack, and once again Richie had to wait, while Mungo ate everything the sack contained and then nosed around, licking up the scattered fragments. His slow thoughts then turned from food to sleep and he settled himself for a nap, his body sprawled in the water while his head rested on the bottom step. Skipper folded the empty sack and slipped it under Mungo's head for a pillow. Only then did he straighten up, ready at last to turn to other things.

This time it was Richie who led the way up the ladder.

"You haven't started building, have you?" he called over his shoulder, shouting the words to make himself heard above the gathering gulls.

" 'Course I haven't. I promised, didn't I?" said

Skipper. "I've just fetched up a few more planks and put my tools out ready."

"I have done something else, though," he added when they reached the shelf. "Look!" And he picked up a knotted-rope hammock and spread it out for Richie to see.

"You mean to say you made it?" marveled Richie. And then, hardly daring to hope what he asked, he whispered: "For me?"

"Aye, for you," said Skipper, smiling. "So now

all we've got to do is build a room to hang it in. There's plenty of space alongside my own cabin."

He had arranged a pile of boxes to form a temporary flight of steps to the roof. Here four stout poles were laid out in readiness with a box full of assorted nails beside them.

"We'll need to fix these uprights first," he explained, rolling up his sleeves.

The job proved to be great fun. It was even better than Richie had expected, because it was a real hard job of work as well as being fun. They soon had the uprights in position, and then Skipper showed how the planks must be arranged.

"They need to overlap like this," he explained. "Then the rain will run off them, see?"

As Skipper held each plank in position, Richie hammered it to the uprights. He quickly learned to use the home-made hammer, and after a couple of false shots he managed to drive the nails securely home without knocking them sideways.

"You've got a real way with that hammer," remarked Skipper approvingly.

"Have I really?" mumbled Richie, flushing with pleasure.

When the walls were a couple of feet high, Skipper suggested breaking off for lunch.

"Already?" cried Richie, who was in no hurry to stop this pleasant work.

"Why not? We've plenty of time to finish the job," said Skipper. "Let's go down and sit with Mungo. He likes a bit of company."

But when they looked into the cavern, Mungo wasn't there.

"Ah well, of course it's low tide and a grand fine day," said Skipper, glancing toward the sea. "I expect we'll find him in his garden."

Turning away from the flowery rocks that Richie thought of as the garden, Skipper started down over the rocks toward the sea. The nearer they got to the water, the fewer flowers there were, and as they passed the final straggling clumps of silverweed, Richie wondered what sort of garden could possibly lie below.

And then he saw it. Just where the rocks dipped into the sea lay an underwater garden bright with jeweled sea anemones spread out like starry flowers. He saw lawns of clear green seaweed and feathery forests lifting and swaying with the movement of the sea while miniature fish darted here and there like water butterflies. And over it all, the gently moving water lay clear as rippled glass.

On the edge of this enchanted spot sprawled Mungo, half in, half out of the water, his eyes closed as he lay basking in blissful peace.

When Richie tried to recall it later, he could never remember that picnic clearly, it seemed like a meal in a dream. He knew he sat on a sun-warmed rock with his bare feet sunk deep in the colored weeds of the pool, their soft fronds warmed by the sunshine through the water. And he remembered the tickle of little fish and prawns as they darted inquisitively around his ankles.

It was not the sort of day for talking and he remembered little of what they ate, apart from a hard-boiled seagull's egg given him by Skipper and some cool, crisp watercress from one of the springs on the Craig. He shared his own picnic lunch with Skipper, who sat contentedly munching sandwiches at his side.

As for Mungo, he opened a lazy eye from time to time, clearly pleased to have them there, but far too comfortable to bother to move across to where they sat.

"He likes basking in the sun even better than being scratched on a day like this," mumbled Skipper, speaking rather indistinctly through a mouthful of home-made chocolate cake.

*Chapter Twelve*

The dream picnic came to an end when Skipper got to his feet with a sudden movement that sent a dozen miniature fish fleeing into the shelter of the nearest seaweed forest. He had had enough of Mungo's garden and was ready to return to work.

"Now for that window!" he remarked, turning his back on the sea.

The window was much harder to fix than the walls, and Skipper tried it this way and that, before he was satisfied and ready to let Richie get to work with his hammer. It was fixed at last, however, and they stood back to admire their handiwork.

"My window," exclaimed Richie happily. "And look how smoothly it opens and shuts," he added, undoing the catch for the twentieth time.

"Just wait till you see the door!" said Skipper.

"I've had it away in the timber cave for years, waiting for a chance to use it. Let's fetch it up." And he led the way over the seaweed thatch and down the stairway of boxes to one of the caves that opened out of his yard.

"There—what about that?" he cried, brushing the dust off a gray door propped up against the wall. The word *Chartroom* was painted across it in bold white letters.

"It must have come off a ship," said Skipper.

They dragged it out and hoisted it up onto the roof between them. Skipper selected screws to fit the hinges, and then, just as they were about to lift it into place, something drew Richie's eyes to the horizon. There, far away still, but coming steadily nearer, was the steamer!

"Oh, why, why, WHY couldn't she just have waited till we'd done the door!" he exploded.

"What does it matter when it's done, one day is as good as another," said Skipper.

"It's all very well for you and Mungo, you've only got the tides to worry about," muttered Richie.

"That's why I like Muckle Craig," said Skipper. "We've got all the time in the world out here. Mungo must have been here for hundreds of years, and as for me, I soon stopped bothering about days and years. What do they matter anyway, they come and go and we can't change them, so why worry?"

Richie thought this conversation over as he rode toward the shore on Mungo's back. Skipper was right, there wasn't any hurry. It was just as much fun doing the job as completing it. So he didn't mind after all when the new room wasn't finished in a hurry. There were even days when they agreed to do no work at all, as on the morning when Richie said, "I've never been right to the top of Muckle Craig."

So up they went to the highest peak, where the sea wind sang among the crags and the sound of the sea was muted to a whisper far below. Richie looked across to the mainland shore and laughed. "Why, the Cliff Hotel looks as small as a dolls' house, and Mrs. Moffatt's croft might be a hen coop!"

"Look at the tide rip. You get a splendid view from here," said Skipper, pointing to the frothing curve of the current where it ran through the calmer sea like a river of tumbling foam.

"Is that little speck the bell buoy?" asked Richie, and when Skipper nodded he remarked: "I can't hear its bell at all from here, can you?"

Eventually, however, in spite of the days when they did no work, the new room was completed.

"We'll put the hammock up tomorrow," promised Skipper.

When Richie woke next morning, however, it was to hear the splash of rain against his bedroom window.

"Why, my dear child, you surely can't want a picnic lunch again today?" exclaimed Aunt Hilda. "Wherever could you find to shelter from this rain?"

But Mrs. Moffatt remembered Angus, and once again she came to Richie's aid. "Oh, I reckon he'll be all right," she said. "Just see he takes his oil-skins, that's all."

Richie felt like a lifeboatman as he rode out to sea with the rain in his face and the water sluicing down the back of his sou'wester.

Skipper was standing on the cavern steps as usual. "Just wait while I feed Mungo and then come up and see," he said, grinning.

"See what?" demanded Richie.

Skipper merely winked, then turned his full attention to the monster. Presently they were on their way up the ladder at last.

As they approached the driftwood house, Richie blinked up at his little window through the rain. "That's funny," he remarked. "My window looks as bright and welcoming in the rain as it does when the sun is shining on the colored glass."

When they reached the chartroom doorway, he saw why and stopped so abruptly that Skipper bumped into his back. For the little window really had gleamed in welcome, because a lighted ship's lantern hung on either side, one with red glass and one with green.

"My port and starboard lanterns," Skipper explained. "I've been waiting years for an excuse to light those up. Not much fun doing it all alone."

Richie now saw that other comforts had been added to his little room. A rope fender, trampled flat, made a neat round mat for the floor, and there were colored rugs in the hammock.

"Get in and see how you like the feel of it," suggested Skipper. Richie needed no urging and immediately threw off his wet oilskins and rolled himself in the rugs in the swinging hammock. He had never before wanted to go to bed in the day-time, and now he wondered when he would ever want to get up again! It was so cozy lying there in the gently swaying hammock, watching the green and crimson lantern light flickering on the ceiling, while the rain hurled itself against his little window.

Presently he became aware of other sounds, quiet rustlings and scratchings. He lifted his head and looked over the edge of the hammock. Skipper was sitting at the table with a sheet of paper spread out in front of him and a colored pencil in each hand.

"Whatever are you doing?" Richie wanted to know.

"Making a chart. No point having a chartroom without any charts. So I'm starting with the tide

rip and the skerries. I'm just going to put in the bell buoy now." And he changed his blue pencil for a red one.

"Wait! Oh, let me help!" cried Richie, rolling out of the hammock in a cascade of colored blankets.

"Sure, help yourself to some pencils," said Skipper as the rain swept in from the sea in a fresh burst of fury.

*Chapter Thirteen*

Everything seemed to come to an end at once. The tranquil summer weather was blotted out by driving rain which came sweeping in from the sea for days on end, then school began, and the timeless holidays were over.

"And the worst of it is, I'll only be free to come over weekends now," Richie explained gloomily to Skipper.

He soon discovered, though, that with the shortening hours of daylight and the ever-changing tides, there were some weekends when he couldn't get across to Muckle Craig at all. He would scramble down to the secret bay as soon as there was light enough to see the way, only to find that he had missed the tide and that Mungo had been and gone.

To make matters worse, Aunt Hilda refused to allow him to have a picnic lunch when the weather was really bad. He might go outdoors if he wanted to, but now that the days were colder she insisted that he must come home for a good hot midday meal. So it was with a heavy heart that he plodded along the cliff one afternoon when the tide was at its lowest. The rain had stopped, but there was a strong, blustery wind, and after battling against it with his head bent low, he was thankful to scramble down into the shelter of his secret bay.

Here he found Mungo's early-morning tracks as he expected, and he flopped down disconsolately beside them. He sat there brooding for a while, scooping up handfuls of damp shingle as

he pictured his gentle old friend lumbering hopefully in from the sea, only to paddle away again
without the expected crisps. He pictured Skipper
waiting just as hopefully out on Muckle Craig,
and suddenly he sprang to his feet and hurled a
handful of shingle far out across the rocks to
relieve his feelings.

It was then that he discovered that he was not
alone on the shore. Someone stood far out on the
rocks, staring at the sea. Although his back was
turned, Richie knew at once that this tall man in
sea boots was a stranger, and in a place where
strangers rarely came. He was not fishing, nor did

he carry a crab hook, so there seemed no reason for him to be standing there among the rocks at the edge of the tide.

Suddenly one of the rocks moved, and there was Mungo rearing up out of the waves, right at the stranger's feet!

Just for a moment Richie froze where he stood, too horrified to move or make a sound. Then he came to his senses and went leaping, scrambling, slithering over the slippery rocks, yelling as he ran: "Go back, Mungo. Back—back—back!"

If Mungo heard, he paid no attention, and went on reaching out toward the stranger with a trustful smile. Richie saw with rising panic that the man was actually giving him something to eat.

Richie was upon them before the stranger heard his voice above the noise of the wind and waves, and when he did turn around he was amazed to see a wild-eyed boy with flailing arms, gasping out as he stumbled forward: "Don't . . . eat it . . . Mungo . . . Drop it . . . It's a bait . . . to trap you . . . He'll only catch you . . . and take you away . . ." And flinging his whole weight against the great beast's side Richie tried to shove him back into the sea. Mungo merely sucked in an untidy fringe of leaves dangling from his smiling mouth and stretched out eagerly for more.

But the tall stranger was looking down at Richie with an unexpectedly friendly smile. And when he spoke, his words were as unexpected as his smile.

"So you know Mungo too! Don't worry, he's my friend and I wouldn't harm him for the world." Then, with a hasty glance toward the cliffs, he said quickly, "You haven't got anyone with you, have you?"

Richie shook his head and the tall man stood studying him thoughtfully for a moment, then said slowly, "Come to think of it, Mom did mention a boy. She said he was off on his own on the cliffs all day and I'd wondered if maybe he'd find Mungo." After a moment's hesitation he went on quietly, "And since you know his name is Mungo, you must know Skipper too."

Richie nodded dumbly, trying to sort out the puzzle. Suddenly part of it fell into place and he looked up with a question. "Then . . . surely . . . you must be Mrs. Moffatt's Angus?"

"I am indeed," said the stranger, smiling broadly.

"There's still something I don't understand," said Richie with a bewildered frown. "Why is Mungo here when the tide is low? I thought he only came across when it was high enough to reach the flowers and grass on the cliff back there."

"True enough," said Angus. "The old fellow comes in to find the foods he cannot find on Muckle Craig, such as those he can pick for himself on the shore and cliffs. But now and then he also comes over for some special treat, brought out to him here on the rocks."

Richie puzzled over this and then demanded, "But how would he know you were here with special food?"

Angus hesitated for a long moment and then said slowly, "Well, since you and I have both stumbled upon the same tremendous secret and discovered the monster, then I think it only fair to tell you my part of the secret. Or rather, I will show you." And putting his hand in his pocket, he pulled out a curious copper object.

"Whatever is it?" asked Richie.

"It's something I found in a rock pool long ago.

I took it to be some sort of a horn, but blow as I would, I could never produce a single note, and I soon lost interest in it.

"And then one day I was sitting out here at low tide, staring across at the Craig and wishing that Mungo would appear and fetch me over, when it occurred to me that if he could be trained to respond to Skipper's bell, then why shouldn't he learn to come to the call of something else as well?

"There was a problem, however. It must be a hidden, secret sound that would not be noticed by anyone who might chance to hear it on the mainland. The sound of Skipper's bell is not very loud by the time it reaches the shore, and it blends with the bell buoy anyway."

"I know, I thought it was the bell buoy when I first heard it," admitted Richie.

"Quite. So I had to find something loud enough for Mungo to hear on Muckle Craig and at the same time soft enough to go unnoticed by anyone who might chance to hear it on the mainland! I wondered if a sound could be sent under water. And then, I don't know why, I suddenly remembered the copper horn found under the water of a rock pool."

"And did it work?" asked Richie, breathlessly.

"It did. I dipped the open end under water and blew, and although I could not hear a thing myself, I saw a string of bubbles flow away under the water to be sucked out to sea on the tide."

"Is it magic, then?" asked Richie, gazing at the horn in his hand.

"I've no idea," said Angus. "I don't understand such things myself.

"Anyway, next time I went to Muckle Craig

I took the horn and Skipper and I tested it together. We couldn't hear the sound ourselves, but it was soon clear that Mungo could—perhaps because he spent all his time in or beside the water. We tried it from farther and farther away, rewarding him with something nice to eat whenever he came lumbering up in answer to the summons. He thought it some delightful kind of game and was always ready to play it.

"It wasn't so easy to train him to come across here, however, and it took months and months to make him understand that when he heard the horn he would find me standing here on the rocks with something good to eat. But once dear old Mungo learns a thing, he never forgets it. It's often weeks between my visits to my mother here, and even then I'm seldom here for long enough to break away and come down to the rocks to see old Mungo. And yet he remembers all through the year and comes over at once when I sound the horn, don't you, old chap?" And he rubbed his hand affectionately over the head still hovering hopefully in front of him.

There was a long silence as Angus continued to

fondle Mungo's head and Richie turned the horn over and over in his hands. After watching him for several minutes, Angus broke the silence.

"Look here," he said. "You have more need of that than I have now. So come along up to the bay and I'll show you where it's kept."

Richie's fingers tightened on the precious object and he looked up speechlessly as Angus went on, "With that horn you can call Mungo any time you like and go out to the Craig whenever you wish, regardless of the state of the tide—always remembering, of course, to bring him some special treat."

"Oh, I always do," said Richie.

"Then you'll be all right. Now this channel here is always deep enough for Mungo, however low the tide. Just follow it out from the little bay and you'll find it's where Mungo will appear in answer to your call.

"No need to thank me," he added as Richie struggled for words. "I shall be only too pleased to think of dear old Skipper enjoying a bit of company, since I can so rarely get across to see him. But maybe one day you and I might ride out there together."

"Couldn't we now?" urged Richie.

"Not today, I've no time, worse luck. Anyhow, come along up and see where I hide the horn."

"What about Mungo?" questioned Richie. "Will he go back on his own without Skipper's bell?"

"Oh yes, once he sees we've got nothing more to give him, he'll be off. There's nothing else for him to linger for out here at low tide. The weed on these rocks is much the same as he'd find on the rocks around the Craig. Here you are, old chap, two last sweets before you go." And he held out a couple of licorice all-sorts on the flat of his hand.

"I never thought of giving him sweets, they seem so small for that great mouth," said Richie.

"Oh, he likes sweets. Tell you something else he likes, and that's a nice toffee apple. Mrs. McFee in the shop always wondered how I could put away so many toffee apples!"

"She'll be wondering the same about me now!" said Richie, hurrying to keep pace with the man's long strides as they made their way back to the secret bay.

The hiding place was a long-disused rabbit burrow overhung with heather half way up the cliff.

"I always wrap it in a leaf or two to keep the dust from getting inside," said Angus, rolling the horn in a dock leaf before thrusting it into the hole. Suddenly he straightened and swung toward the sea.

"Here she comes!" he cried, pointing to a small black speck on the horizon. Then with a sudden laugh he added: "I'm forgetting that my day is no longer bounded by the passing of the yellow-funneled steamer! And yet I really believe those were the best days I ever had. Anyway, I must be getting back to my lighthouse now, and no doubt you must be back for your tea before the steamer passes out of sight."

"And tomorrow," cried Richie rapturously, "tomorrow I'll try the copper horn!"

Chapter Fourteen

When Richie woke in the dark next morning, he wondered if it had all been a dream. Had he really met Angus on the rocks and been shown the secret that would enable him to cross to Muckle Craig whenever he wished? He jumped out of bed and ran across to the window and there was the lighthouse flinging its four quick flashes over the sea as usual. The light was real and Angus was real, so why shouldn't the secret horn be real as well?

It seemed as though the daylight would never come, but at last he was hurrying along the cliff-top path. One of his pockets bulged with a toffee apple, its wooden stick catching his hand as he ran.

When he reached the secret bay, he was almost afraid to look behind the heather. But the burrow was there, just as he remembered it. He reached

inside and felt the leaf-wrapped bundle where
Angus had hidden it.

The gully was easily seen and he followed it
out to where the low tide was feeling its way
between the rocks. He chose a spot where he
could kneel on a flat stone and dip the open end
of the horn into deep water below. Then, bending
down, he put his lips to the mouthpiece and blew.

A long string of bubbles streamed out under the water and before they could rise to the surface they were sucked out to sea in the undertow.

He wondered how long it would take the bubbles to flow across to Muckle Craig and whether Mungo would really be awake enough to respond. He wondered, too, how long it would take the beast himself to swim across the half mile of turbulent sea that lay between the Craig and the mainland shore.

Slipping the horn into his pocket, he settled down with his arms clasped around his knees to wait. But he didn't sit still for long, there was too much to see.

There appeared to be more life out here than higher up the shore, and everything seemed to be on the move, as though making the most of this brief spell of air and sunlight between the tides. Winkles and even slow-moving limpets were creeping about the rocks, while crabs scuttled around below in search of food. He was soon bent double, watching a timid hermit crab venturing nervously across a foot of open ground between the weed-forested walls of a quiet pool.

Something bumped him from behind, almost toppling him head first into the pool. Clutching the rock to regain his balance, he swung around to find Mungo nuzzling at his pocket.

"Oh, good old Mungo, how quick you've been!" he exclaimed. Then, with a laugh, he added, "Oh, I see what you're after. Wait then, while I pull it out for you." And he dragged the toffee apple from his pocket and held it out to the great beast.

Mungo sucked it in with a single gulp and chumbled it up with a great deal of noise, the stick poking out in front and waggling up and down as he chewed.

"Here, let me take that stick," suggested Richie, but Mungo jerked his head aside and refused to part with it.

"It looks awfully funny sticking out like that. Am I going for a ride on a swordfish or what?" asked Richie as he took his seat on the monster's back.

The tide rip ran close to the rocks at low water, and Mungo soon plowed through it. He was already heading in toward the cavern entrance when he suddenly lifted his head, seeming to sniff the air.

"Whatever's up?" questioned Richie. And then he caught a whiff himself, a faint hint of wood-smoke, like the smell of a picnic fire.

Mungo promptly altered course, and instead of entering the cavern, he skirted the base of the precipice, rounding the high end of the Craig and following the coastline up the other side.

Richie wondered why they had not gone in to see Skipper first, but he had learned that nothing would alter Mungo's course once his mind was set on something.

The cliffs continued tall and sheer, with here and there a narrow inlet.

"Oh, Mungo, what a great place!" Richie cried. "I've never seen this side of Muckle Craig before —except from above, when Skipper and I looked down from the top, up there among the crags."

Presently the cliffs fell back to form a little bay of fine white sand from which a thin trail of smoke rose up against the pink cliffs. A driftwood fire was blazing in a roughly constructed stone fireplace in the middle of the beach. A covered saucepan was balanced over the flames and a scarlet mug stood on a rock beside the fire. The beach appeared to be deserted.

The white sand shelved so steeply into the deep green water that Mungo was able to paddle close inshore. Richie slid from his back and stood looking about him.

A figure wandered into sight at the far end of the bay. As it drew nearer, Richie saw that it was Skipper looking like some gnome from a fairy tale as he ambled slowly along the tide line, bent double under a large sack into which he collected driftwood as he came.

At sight of him, Mungo slapped the water with his tail, sending a sudden wave running up the sand. As it swept toward him, Skipper pounced on a piece of driftwood and snatched it up before it could be washed away out of his reach. As he did so, he called out: "That you, Mungo?"

Richie grinned, remembering the first time he had heard Skipper say those words. "I thought he was speaking a different language," he recalled.

Skipper now heaved up his sack and glanced

along the beach, expecting to see Mungo. When he caught sight of Richie standing there, he looked almost as astonished as he had looked that first day in the cavern. But his astonishment soon widened into a delighted grin, and he shouted: "However did you get here at low tide?"

As they hurried toward one another, Richie told of his meeting with Angus, and Skipper nodded slowly as Richie brought the horn out of his pocket to show him.

"Ah," said Skipper, "so that's the way of it. Well, I hoped that maybe one day something of the kind might happen. So now you'll be able to come out here often, winter, summer, low tide and high," he went on happily, swinging the sack from his shoulder and turning it upside down. A pile of treasure from the tide line poured out onto the sand. Most of it was driftwood for the fire, but there were some other useful odds and ends as well. Skipper stooped to pick up a blue mug.

"Lucky I happened to find this in time for our meal," he remarked. "Will you wash it in the sea while I see to the fire?"

"Aye, aye, sir," said Richie. He skipped down to

the edge of the water where Mungo lay peacefully sleeping, his head cradled on the sand while the sea lapped around his body, which lay spread-eagled under the clear water.

He got back to find Skipper feeding the fire with pieces of driftwood that hissed into life in flames of blue and green.

"Like Mungo's colors, only much much brighter," commented Richie.

Skipper got up and lifted the lid of the sauce-pan and a strange smell mingled with the tang of woodsmoke.

"What is it?" asked Richie, stepping closer to sniff inquiringly.

"Oh, seaweed mostly, and a bit of shellfish, winkles and that, with a couple of pinches of thyme and samphire."

Richie was silent. He had never eaten any of these things and he didn't like the sound of them at all. However, Skipper obviously had no doubts and was already tipping a generous helping of the mixture into the scarlet mug that he handed to Richie before turning back to fill the blue one for himself.

They sat down on the sand and Richie held his mug between his hands, making a show of blowing

on the contents as he sniffed them warily, putting off the moment when he must taste them.

Surprisingly, it wasn't bad at all. By the second cautious sip he decided it was quite nice, and by the time he tipped back his head to drain the last drops from the bottom it was so delicious that he was delighted when Skipper peered into the saucepan and reported that there was enough for a second helping each.

Skipper sat back with a sigh of deep contentment.

"Now I'll be able to show you every single bit of Muckle Craig," he said happily.

"I know—I know!" cried Richie. "And the secret adventure will go on and on forever, because nobody knows it's possible to land on Muckle Craig."

"And nobody knows that somebody actually lives out here in a driftwood house," added Skipper.

"With a real live monster on the doorstep," finished Richie.

They thought that Mungo was asleep, but to show that he was wide awake he suddenly joined in the conversation by bringing his tail down *slap* on the water, sending an unexpected wave surging up the beach, and opening one green eye to watch Richie and Skipper roll laughing backward out of reach as it hissed among the embers of their fire.